Smile, Sophia

Skylaar Amann

FEIWEL AND FRIENDS
NEW YORK

yummy plants?

sauropod
- long neck
- long tail
- eats plants

Raar!!

theropod
- meat-eaters
- 3 fingers
- walk on 2 feet

m. scowlosaurus??

?

~~ornithians~~
ornithiscians
- eat plants
- beak-like snout
- some have horns

A Feiwel and Friends Book ⋆ An imprint of Macmillan Publishing Group, LLC ⋆ 120 Broadway, New York, NY 10271 ⋆ mackids.com ⋆ Copyright © 2022 by Skylaar Amann. All rights reserved. ⋆ Our books may be purchased in bulk for promotional, educational, or business use. Please contact your local bookseller or the Macmillan Corporate and Premium Sales Department at (800) 221-7945 ext. 5442 or by email at MacmillanSpecialMarkets@macmillan.com. ⋆ Library of Congress Cataloging-in-Publication Data is available. First edition, 2022 ⋆ Book design by Lisa Vega ⋆ The artwork was created with pencil and Photoshop Feiwel and Friends logo designed by Filomena Tuosto ⋆ Printed in China by R.R. Donnelley, Asia Printing Solutions Limited. ⋆ ISBN 978-1-250-81695-5 (hardcover)

1 3 5 7 9 10 8 6 4 2

For all the girls who only
smile when they want to

Sophia was smart. Sophia was strong.
And Sophia was really good
at digging holes.

But no one cared.
Everyone just wanted
Sophia to smile.

Sophia knew a lot about shark teeth.
And old fossils.

And strange, hard-to-find,
mysterious bones.
Like the ones from the
Megalodontis scowlosaurus.

M. Scowlosaurus?

Sophia was happiest when she was searching
for the bones of her favorite dinosaur.

But she wasn't going to smile just because the grown-ups told her to.

"I'll smile when I want to," Sophia said.

"The only tool you need right now
is a pretty smile!" sang her mother.
But Sophia did not smile.

"Oh no, I forgot about picture day!"
cried Sophia when she got to school.

"Smile, Sophia!" said Mr. Blecky.
"No one likes an angry girl!"
He didn't understand dinosaur
researchers at all.

"I'm not angry," said Sophia, but she couldn't think of a good enough reason to smile. Photos were boring anyway, unless they were pictures of dinosaur bones.

At the science fair, Sophia set up her project.
Dioramas made her happy.
Especially the ones with dinosaurs.

But all her teacher noticed
was Sophia's face. "SMILE!"
Miss Primm called out. "We must
welcome our audience!"

"There's more to science than
smiling!" said Sophia. "Like adding
to the collective knowledge of the
world, for example!"

After school, the grown-ups' demands ran through Sophia's mind.

"The only tool you need is a smile!" her mother sang.

"Smile for the camera!" said Mr. Blecky.

"Welcome the audience with a smile!" called Miss Primm.

"I'll smile when
I have something
worth
smiling about!"
Sophia shouted.

Sophia ran to her dig site.
Nothing made her feel better than digging for dinosaurs.
But still, Sophia did not smile.

After all,
paleontology was
serious business.

So Sophia dug and
dug and dug.

Until her shovel hit
something hard.

It was an old,
dirty, crooked, weird,
strange, elegant,
beautiful jawbone.

"Eureka!" shouted Sophia.

"It's the majestic mandible of the
Megalodontis scowlosaurus!"

The *Megalodontis scowlosaurus* was known for being smart. And strong.

And really good at digging holes. Sophia thought it was fascinating.

new evidence.

No scientist had ever found a complete
Megalodontis scowlosaurus jawbone before.
But now, Sophia had.

So then—only for herself
and that majestic mandible of the
Megalodontis scowlosaurus—
Sophia smiled.

Can you find it?

There are lots of creatures, fossils, and other scientific things hidden in this book's illustrations. Can you find them? Here is a little bit of information about some of these, but if you look closely at the pages of this book, you might find even more!

Amber: Fossilized tree resin that sometimes has something, like an insect, preserved inside. Amber can give scientists a window into the past.

***Parasaurolophus*:** Known for the distinctive crest on its head. This may have helped it smell, make sounds to communicate, or show off to other dinos.

Charles Darwin: Famous for his theory of evolution. Darwin mostly studied living creatures, while paleontologists study fossils. Both help us understand our world. Oddly, there's no record of anyone asking Charlie to smile.

***Tyrannosaurus* skull:** *T. rex* had 60 teeth, used to crush its meals. But scientists aren't sure if *T. rex* was a hunter or scavenger (or both!), despite it often being portrayed as a mighty fighter.

***Archaeopteryx*:** A bird-like dinosaur with wings, feathers, claws, and teeth. Because it looks similar to both birds and dinosaurs, this creature helps explain the origin of birds and how they relate to dinosaurs.

Triceratops: Known for its three big horns and bird-like beak. Despite its tough appearance, it actually ate plants. The big guy could weigh up to 16,000 pounds and be 30 feet long!

Mary Anning: A trailblazing paleontologist who discovered the first *Ichthyosaurus* (an ancient "fish-lizard") fossil in the early 1800s. Despite men trying to keep Mary out of science, she persevered. History is hazy on the matter, but this author suspects Mary only smiled when she wanted to.

Ammonite: A type of extinct creature closely related to nautiluses, octopuses, and squids. You can often see a distinct spiral shape in these fossils—or models of them.

The Daily Fossil

Megalodon tooth: One of the biggest fish to swim the earth, with huge teeth to match. We learn a lot from shark teeth because they survive much longer than cartilage. Megalodon actually means "big tooth"—its teeth can be over six inches long.

Tiktaalik roseae: Actually a fish, not a dinosaur. But this "fishapod" is very special because it could prop itself up on its fins—almost like a land animal! All tetrapods (amphibians like frogs and even humans) are descended from *Tiktaalik*.

The paleontologist's tool kit